The Other Girl

Horror thriller screen play

Vinod Narayanan

NYNA BOOKS
www.nynabooks.com

English Language
The other girl
(Screen play)
Vinod Narayanan
Rights Reserved

First Malayalam print Edition: November 2019
First English print Edition: May 2022

ISBN: 9798832042534

Cover & Typesetting: Boons Entertainments

Published by
NYNA BOOKS
MSME/UAN Regd. KL07D0004957
www.nynabooks.com
Email: nynabooks@gmail.com

Vinod Narayanan

Vinod Narayanan is an Indian author. He was born on March 24, 1975 at Thripunithura in Ernakulam district, Kerala state in India. His father Chottanikkara Velumbarambil Narayanan and his mother Thrippunithura Eroor Vaniyathuparambil Omana. He studied in Chottanikkara Govt Arts College and Thripunithura Govt College. After graduating in history he became a journalist. Now he is an independent writer and screenwriter. Five short films were scripted and screened in various international film Festivals and won awards.

The first novel 'Mayakkottaram' (The Magic Palace) was published in 1999 at

Manorajyam weekly. He has published forty short stories in different periodicals. More than 160 books have been published by various publishers. The main books are "The Red" (novel), "Double murder" (Novel), Mandarayakshi (Novel), Mumbai Restaurant (Novel), Nayika (Novel), Kamika (Novel), Welcome to Kochi (Novel) and other Malayalam books. Black night gown (Film script), Incest (Stories), the imagination of secret lover (Stories), Talking birds (Stories) are his English fictions. Also he wrote 60 children's books.

Address:
'Sivaranjani'
Chempu. P.O, PIN: 686608
Vaikom, Kottayam district,
Kerala state, India
Phone: 9567216134
Email: boonsenter@gmail.com

The living and the dead spirits will travel with us without the biological nerve of the body, moving along the path of the illusion of the mind. Many people know the presence of spirits in many ways. The Magical World is haunted by the phenomenon of modern science being called the duel personality. This psychological suspense horror thriller screenplay seeks to answer the question whether the ghost is a tricky or real thing about human mind.

The Other Girl

Scene - 1

Daytime

Interior.

A cell of the human mental asylum. There were white painted walls and doors. A girl feared isolated within the cell. The appearance of the 17-year-old girl is, wearing a white colored long gown. The loose hair hides the face.

Two nurses of the mental health center came and opened the door of the cell. They enter, and there is no motion to the girl. She does not try to look at them.

Nurses had little worry. Both took hold of the girl. She is like a doll. Nurses are carried out by the girl.

Nurse: "Come on..."

*****

Scene - 2

Daytime

Interior.

Nurses walked with the girl through the hallway. White paint covered the corridor. In front of the camera shot, a woman of 30 year old follows the girl and nurses just behind them. In makeup, she looks like a ghost. The woman follows the girl and looks stare her. The girl understands that the woman is in behind, she suddenly stood there. Her eyes are with unsolved eyesight between the hairs.

She looked back. There is no one.

Nurses hold her tight.

Nurse: "walk."

Walking continues.

Camera shot from the back. The girl often turns to the fear.

*****

Scene - 3

Daytime

Interior.

Nurses brought the girl to a big room. The walls and doors of the room covered with white paint. There were a white table and two chairs in the middle of the room. Nurses set the girl on the chair and they went out. The girl is hiding her face with the hair and her head is hunched. When the camera zooms towards the girl is zoomed out, there is a woman on the chair across her. That respected woman was Dr. Veny.

Dr. Veny: "Devika?"

 The girl does not raise her head.

Dr. Veny: "Devika ... look at it"

The girl does not raise her head.

Dr. Veny: "Come on baby ... Devika ...look at me ... I'm Veny .... Doctor Veny ..."

The girl raises her head and looks at her.

Dr. Veny: "Good. Good girl ... good morning! ... Did you sleep well yesterday? ... "

The girl looks silently watching the doctor.

Dr. Veny: "Tell me ... Devika"

The girl said, "Uum ..."

Dr. Veny: "Do you have the breakfast?"

The girl has been taking too much time to reply.

Dr. Veny: "Devika, Do you remember what day is today?"

Devika bowed her head.

With the muscles on the face appearing through half of the hair follicles, that mind is going through some way.

The woman who followed the girl in the hallway is now sitting in the doctor's position. Her face is angry and disgusting.

She suddenly felt that the opposite was another woman who was sitting in the chair. Devika shocked her head. Close up.

The next shot, Doctor Veny is sitting on the chair. The relief is on the face of Devika

Dr.Veny: "What about you? Why are you shocked?" (Relief). You did not answer me what I asked. "

Devika is watching the doctor with apathy.

Dr. Veny continued with a smile.

Dr. Veny: "Today is the seventeenth birthday of Devika. Your father is coming. He called me in the morning. "

Now camera can show that ghost woman is standing behind Devika.

Devika understands that she is behind her.

She turns back in the next shot.

There is nothing.

 The place is empty.

Dr. Veny: "What..... What happened you Devika?"

She is murmuring with fear: "I saw ... something ... like ... that Devil Lady ..."

Dr. Veny: "Who..?"

Girl said with a feeling that everyone knows:"Lady ... in the ... black gown ..."

Dr. Veny: "Vasundhara ....your mom ...?"

Suddenly the girl is shivering (in fearful manner): "She is not my mom."

The doctor's face was alert.

After a while, Dr. Veny: "She was dead, Devika!"

Girl (in scary manner): "Yah... but her ghost is alive ..."

The doctor's face faded.

Mobile started to ring.

Dr. Veny took the mobile.

Dr. Veny (to Devika): "Devika's father calling. (She is attending the phone). Have you come to the office? ... Please wait ... We will come to you ..."

After the phone call the doctor got up and called the nurse.

Dr. Veny: "Shosha ..."

Nurses are coming.

Dr. Veny: "Change her dress and refresh her."

The doctor is going.

Nurses turn towards Devika.

*****

Scene - 4

Daytime

Interior.

Doctor Veny's Consulting Room.

Devika's father Indrakumar and Veny. Indrakumar is a handsome man who is about 40 years old.

Indra Kumar (with sadness) said: "Is there any hope for her?

Dr. Veny: "She does not show her violence now. But that does not change the apathy. "

Indra Kumar: "Shall I take her out to show the city and the park?"

Dr. Veny: "No. No sight is present in her eyes or minds. Another problem is she feels that Vasundhara's ghost hunts her up. "

Indra Kumar: "Doctor ... but ..."

Dr. Veny: "The darkness which has undertaken her consciousness has not departed."

Indra Kumar (sadly): "My daughter... Did she not return to me doctor?"

At that time, Devika comes with the help of nurses. Her hair is tied up. The dress has changed. Nevertheless, the feeling of fear and appearance is on the face.

Dr. Veny: "Ah... Daughter came ... come on Devika..."

They placed Devika on the chair.

Indra Kumar: "Daughter ...!"

Devika does not react. She has a pale, motionless, vague face.

Dr. Veny: "Don't you hear your father?"

Indra Kumar: "Daughter …?"

Devika is responding after a while. Horrifying speech: "I don't want talk to anybody …"

She rose up like a doll.

Nurses took her away. As she walks out of the room, she saw, Vasundhara is standing near the doorway of the corridor. Vasundara was talking in the phone. Devika stopped walking with jolt.

Then she went back a bit and looks back once again to Vasundhara (Vasundhara is not in the frame. Devika is looking at the camera)

Her face changed. She threw out the hands of nurses. She cried aloud.

Dr. Veny and Indrakumar came by running.

*****

Scene - 5

Daytime

Car ride.

Devika is traveling in the back seat of her car. Now she is a beautiful girl.

She's enjoying the beautiful views of outside.

Indrakumar is driving the car.

In the next camera shot, there comes Bhadra near to Devika.

Bhadra also is a beautiful girl of seventeen. But Devika is more handsome than Bhadra.

Indra Kumar (with cheerfulness): "Do you know about the specialty of today?"

Devika (with joy): "We are coming home."

Indus Kumar: "It's not just ..!"

Devika (with ecstasy): "Then ..?

Indrakumar: "Today is your birthday. Is it forgotten ...?

Devika: "Oh sweet daddy... together let's go to the temple in the evening."

Indrakumar takes a tin of chocolate from the dashboard of the car and given it to Devika.

Devika bought it.

Bhadra snatched it from Devika's hands.

Bhadra: "Ayyady ... this is all you need ..."

Devika: "Dad, Do you see this?"

Indra Kumar: "I will give you the rest of the gift later ..."

*****

Scene - 6

Daytime

The car came in front of a beautiful house.

It was a renovated old Nalukettu Kerala style house.

It has the beauty of a resort, lonely place.

Indrakumar comes out of the car.

He opened the dickey of the car and took out the bag and boxes outside. Devika and Bhadra came out by enjoying the beauty of the house and the surroundings. Devika ran to the corner of the yard. There is a swing cot. She sat on it and hanged on. Bhadra runs to another place. There are small concrete ponds in the plot. She went to see the small fishes in the pond.

Devika is running with the smile.

Hear the call of Indrakumar. : "Daughter ..?"

Both run towards the call of father.

They passed out the Padippura (door) and walked through the Nadumuttam (courtyard).

Both of them were shocked by seeing the woman in front.

It is mother Vasundhara (the ghost found in the hospital).

They have come with juice in two glasses.

Vasundhara (with fondly): "mole (Daughter)..."

The faces of Devika and Bhadra were darkened in anger.

Vasundhara (with tenderness): "What happened you my dear?"

Devika fended the juice with anger.

Vasundhara shocked and stood as a struck hit on her face.

Devika and Bhadra rushed into the room with anger.

Vasundhara stood with anger staring at the direction they went to. Then she sat down and picked up the glass pieces from the floor.

Then Indrakumar came there.

Indrakumar: "What's the matter?"

Vasundhara (with angry): "It's your daughter did this... She does not want my juice.

Indra Kumar: "No matter, let's go."

He is also helping her to get glass pieces from the floor.

*****

Scene - 7

Daytime

Interior.

Devika's Bed room.

Devika is checking her things...She opens the shelves, opens the table, checking book shelf.

Bhadra picked up a drawing book by the time. She's sitting on the bed and looking at old drawings. Devika also joins her.

Then someone knocks at the door.

"Dum...dum...dumm"

Devika is listening carefully and looking at Bhadra gingerly.

Then Devika got up in the slack. She opened the door.

No one was outside the room.

She got back in the room.

Devika (to Bhadra with disgust):"It may be that ugly woman."

Bhadra finds something in the compound. Devika is looking at that part through the small window. There Vasundhara is doing something in the garden.

Devika and Bhadra looked at each other.

At that time they heard someone calling from the Thody (compound).

Devika went to the window. She looked down to the compound.

Indra Kumar was bathing in the pond of the compound. He looked at the window and called Devika.

Devika happily gets out of the room by holding Bhadra's hand.

As she got out of the way, she saw through the open door, Vasundhara is doing something in the room.

That woman was in another dress.

Devika's face crinkled with suspicion.

Bhadra pulled her hand.

Both of them fled to the ground.

Camera is focus to Vasundhara.

Vasundhara looks at the camera with angry, as an appearance of a ghost.

*****

Scene - 8

Daytime

Pond in the compound.

Indrakumar is bathing. Devika and Bhadra came down to the pond with curiosity.

Indra Kumar: "How is this pool?"

Devika, enjoying the beauty of the old pond: "I thought my dad could have covered this pond."

Indra Kumar: "When I came to buy this land, I have decided that the pool was the first thing to cover. But I did not do it. It is the legacy of our ancestors.

There is a good bath in this pond. It is not about anywhere else ..."

Indra Kumar (looking at Bhadra): "you ... come on."

Devika was looking at it. Bhadra went down to the pond. Indrakumar hold Bhadra's hand to get down to the pond. Her legging and top were drenched in water.

Indrakumar and Bhadra tied each other and playing in water. Devika looks at it. She does not like it. Indraskumar's touch on Bhadra is not just like a daughter.

 Devika becomes upset.

*****

Scene - 9

Daytime

Indra Kumar got out of the pond and walked at home.

His body was wet and wet. A wet dog also runs in front.

Devika is walking behind him.

She looked at him with unhappy.

Bhadra is walking with Devika.

 Bhadra smiled at something in mind. She was not wet.

Then Indra kumar turned around and looked at Bhadra and laughed.

Devika looks at both with furious anger.

Indra Kumar goes home. The dog suffused the water. It goes to the courtyard.

Bhadra is shoving an old ladies cycle from the corner of yard.

 Bhadra tries to drive it.

But the cycle is not going forward. It was stubborn with old.

Devika (mocked): "Fool, this is rusty in years."

Bhadra abandoned bicycle with despair.

Both of them went inside the home.

*****

Scene - 10

Daytime

Interior.

Devika and Bhadra are going to the room.

Devika listened to a room. And from there she heard murmurings and giggles.

She looked through the door gap.

Indra Kumar and Vasundhara are hugging each other with lust.

Bhadra (looking at the shoulder of Devika): "What's up there?"

Devika (She prevents Bhadra from seeing it): "The spear! Bull shit ... comes here ..."

Devika yanked Bhadra.

Both of them went upstairs.

*****

Scene - 11

Daytime

Interior.

They pushed the door of the bedroom. Devika and Bhadra entered the room. Bhadra goes to the bathroom.

Devika is upset.

She is looking out for a while through the window.

When looking at the transparent water jug on the table, there is no water.

She went out of the room with the jug.

*****

Scene - 12

Daytime

Interior.

Devika comes slowly with the water jug.

She looked around and went to the fridge, opened it and filled the water jug. She did not drink water.

Devika was going back.

From the parent's room she heard murmurings, whiz and giggles.

She listened to it.

She looked through the door gap.

She saw her dad Indra Kumar and Vasudhara, who were in sex in the bedroom.

Devika flummoxed.

Unknowingly, the water jug fluctuated from her hand. Water floated on the floor.

Vasundhara heard the sound of falling water, she was shocked. She looked at the door.

Devika was shifted from the door.

Water jug fell down from her hand.

Devika ran away from there.

******

Scene - 13

Daytime

Interior.

Devika's Bedroom.

Bhadra comes out of the bathroom.

She drinks water from the jug (the same water jug of Devika) on the table near the window.

While Bhadra drinking water from the jug Devika opened the door and ran inside and the door is shut.

She is panting.

"What's up?"

Bhadra asked in sign language.

Devika's gesture shows that she does not have anything to say.

She has not been able to stop panting.

She wrested the jug from Bhadra's hand.

She drinks water hungrily from the jug.

*****

Scene - 14

Daytime

Interior.

Vasundhara's room.

Vasundhara is engaged in sex with Indra Kumar.

She sits over Indra Kumar and makes sex. In the meanwhile, she got angry and looked at the door.

She understood that someone looked at them.

Vasundhara jumped off from the body of Indrakumar.   He does not understand anything.

Vasundhara heaps her dress by hiding her nakedness and comes to the door.

Indra Kumar: "What?"

Vasundhara: "Somebody seems to be looking. She will be. I heard the sound of the water falling. "

There is no water in the floor at the door.

Vasundhara: "But I do not see water here?"

Indra Kumar: "If so, you will have imagined it. Lock the door. "

She locked the door of the room, with pettish.

And she murmured: "You have sex with me without locking the door of the room.

Did she see that? "

Indra Kumar: "It does not."

She came and sat on the bed. He is going to touch her. Vasundhara raised his hand and moved.

Vasundhara: "Sit away ..."

Indra Kumar is sitting in shame.

Indra Kumar: "If she sees our sex, it will be indelicacy. But ... oh no... The entire mood was thrown away. "

Both of them were idle and sat in bed.

*****

Scene - 15

Daytime

Exterior.

Devika and Bhadra read the books sitting on the chairs in the verandah.

Bhadra read a picture story and she is laughing.

She shows it to Devika.

Devika laughs at reading that book.

Indra Kumar comes. His dress is Bermuda and T-shirt.

He happily said, "I will show you a canon."

She looked at him with angry.

Her eyes touched his whole body.

Indra Kumar understood it. There was a slight shame in him.

Bhadra got up with joy. Induskumar's shame disappeared.

Bhadra turned to Devika and showed her a sign to come. Bhadra happily goes with Indra Kumar.

*****

Scene - 16

Daytime

Exterior.

Indra Kumar took Bhadra to the cage of love birds. Devika were back in distance.

Indrakumar and Bhadra were nuzzling birds. Devika also is coming along.

She forgets the melancholy.

Indrakumar says: "This is my special pet. Do you know what the name of it is? "

Bhadra and Devika are looking deliberately.

Indrakumar looks them curiously.

Devika (Pleasantly): "Devu ..!"

Indra Kumar: "Bhadra."

Bhadra: "hay ..."

Bhadra hugged Indra Kumar.

Indra Kumar hoisted and flourished her in the air.

Devika's face became dark with anger.

She stared at that love bird in the cage.

She turned a few feet back and stop with hatred. The camera is centered on Devika

Indrakumar's face was almost as touching the face of Devika.

Indra Kumar (fondly): "What's the matter with my daughter? Give me a kiss."

Devika (forbiddingly): "Who is Dad's special pet?"

Indra Kumar is touching the lips of Devika: "My dearest daughter..."

Devika (breakthrough): "And why is that bird named Bhadra?"

Indra Kumar: "What are you saying?"

Bhadra coddling the love birds standing near the cage.

Devika pointed Bhadra and said to Indrakumar: "I do not like anyone to love her, because I love her. Let no one love her except myself. "

Induskumar is petrified.

Devika walked away.

******

Scene - 17

At night.

Interior.

Vasundhara takes dinner at the dining table.

Dinner is served in three plates.

Vasundhara calling when the food is served: "Molay ..?"

Devika and Bhadra came to eat with turgid faces.

Vasundhara: "Where is your father?"

Devika was looking at Vasundhara with disdain.

Devika took curry and poured in the rice.

Bhadra was in front of meals. She looks forward to both.

Vasundhara is watching Devika, as if she does not like her acts.

Devika does not like what Vasundhara outface her. She is frequently looking at Vasundhara with stare.

Vasundhara (looking at the door and told to Indrakumar): "Do not you come to dinner...Ho ... call dinner and call and walk after ..."

Devika is eating meals as anything does not affect herself.

Bhadra is eating incredulously.

Vasundhara did not start eating meals. She is looking steady at Devika.

When Devika is looking for two or three times, Vasundhara is watching Devika. Devika was angry.

She took the food plate and throws it to the face of Vasundhara. Vasundhara took bath in the rice and curry. She was shocked.

Devika got up and tried to go out, Vasundhara hold her securely. Vasundhara slapped her cheeks.

Vasundhara: "You're so arrogance?"

Then she beats Devika gruffly.

Vasundhara: "I have forgiven you for coming recently. Do you rule me?

Bhadra stopped eating food and watching these acts.

Indrakumar ran up. He yanked and shunted vasundhara.

Indra Kumar (To Vasundhara): "What's this ..?"

Vasundhara (pointed to food waste on her body): "Do not see this ..."

Devika is going with unabashed.

And Bhadra goes too.

*****

Scene - 18

At night.

Interior.

The bedroom of Devika.

Devika and Bhadra are lying on a bed thoroughly lights out.

The light comes through the window.

Horrible situation.

Camera focus on the face of Devika.

Scary muscles in the face.
Devika's mind is gripping into a dream.

*****

Scene - 19

At night.
Interior.

Devika's bedroom.

The dream of Devika.
Devika and Bhadra are sleeping on the bed.
Only a muggy moon light from the window.
There have a horrible situation.
Bhadra produced a horrible sound. Her eyes are closed.
Someone is sexually harassing Bhadra.
The guy is not visible.
Bhadra's head, moves towards the sexual rhyme.
She is screaming with pain.

******

Scene - 20

At night.
Interior.

The bedroom of Devika
(Continuity of the scene 18.)

The close up shot of the face of Devika

She suddenly woke up from the sleep. The camera is gradually wider.

Devika is looking for Bhadra on the bed. She is not in bed.

The moonlight has comes through the window.

Devika is rising up in hurry.

Suddenly, the door of the bedroom seems to be open gently. Devika looked at there.

In the dark, the door was just closed, without putting bolt. It opens slowly. There have a fearing environment.

Devika lay slowly on her bed, with fear.

She has covered with the blanket.

She stopped a few moments of breath. Then she changed the blanket from her face.

She looked into the dark. In the dark, someone sprawl on knees through the floor. It prowls and approaches her.

Devika was watching it with shock.

She is not even able to move on with fear. She can't make any noise by fear.

At the foot of the cot, she saw that dark figure. The vague shape is a fright woman dressed in black night gown.

The very moment, the fright dark shape entered on the top of the bed and the legs stood stride on both sides of Devika's legs.

Though the face is not clear, the shape is similar to Vasundhara.

Now the fright dark shape placed its legs on the both side of Devika's haunch.

The fright's black night gown's fringe spreads on the body of Devika.

At the next moment, the fright dark shape was fixed her legs on the both sides of the chest of Devika.

Devika was afraid and looked up.

The fright looks like a mountain that stands up in front of her eyes.

The frightening of the shape of the form came forward. Black Gown covered the face of Devika. She felt suffocation.

Darkness.

The next moment she shook her head and got up.

No unaccustomed things in the bedroom.

But Bhadra is not in the bedroom.

Devika got up. She got the switch of light, but she refused to put on.

Then she opened the door of the bedroom. She steps down the stairs so slowly. Murky light everywhere.

The silence is as all are asleep.

Devika came to the hall and observed the rooms. She saw the door of Vasundhara's room a little open.

She walked slowly and came to that room.

Vasundhara's room was empty.
Disgust was evident in her face.

******

Scene - 21

At night.

Interior.

Bedroom of Devika

There have no light.

It's just half the moonlight from the window. The cots are empty.

In half a light, the door of the bathroom is opened.

The bathroom is not lighted.

Bhadra comes out from the bathroom. She locked the door of the bathroom.

As if she had done something mysterious, she came to her bed with hitched hair and sat on the bed. Then she lies on the bed with a long respiration.

******

Scene - 22

At night.

Interior.

Hall.

Darkness.

It's just half the light from the window.

Devika realized that Vasundhara was not in her room.

Then she searched there.

She stopped near a window.

There was gloomy moon light.

Devika is looking at something in the garden bench. The shadows are moving.

Two people were in the bench.

Devika opened the hall's door slowly. She sneaked and walked to the garden.

*****

Scene - 23

At night.

Garden.

There was moonlight.

Vasundhara and Indrakumar were in love in the garden bench. They were doing open sex with enthusiasm. Indrakumar moved over her with the sexy rhythm.

Vasundhara's black night gown is almost untied.

Devika is watching this from the darkness of the verandah.

******

Scene - 24

At night.

Interior.

Kitchen.

On the dull light, one hand is searching something through the slabs in the kitchen. It was a gauntlet black hand.

It was a hand with a black gown.

It searched and chose a knife.

When the knife took in the hand, a spoon falls down.

Still the shape of the person is not clear.

*****

Scene - 25

At night.

Garden.

Devika is in the verandah near the garden.

She heard the fallen sound of the spoon.

She shocked and became so concentrated.

As she walked back, she turned and looked at Vasundhara and Indrakumar who were in garden bench.

Vasundhara looked at her and secretly smiled with the hidden malice.

Devika walked quickly to the hall.

******

Scene - 26

At night.

Interior.

Devika walks through the hall.

She goes to the kitchen.

In the gloomy light, Devika sees a part of the black night gown moving through the kitchen.

She was shocked.

She approached the door with trembling.

A dark fright stands inside the kitchen.

It stands there with a shiny knife.

The furrow of the knife is shining in the light that comes through the window.

That fright dark shape is similar to Vasundhara.

That is what Devika faced in the bedroom.

She noticed that it is going with the knife to target someone.

She looked at there.

There is another person inside the kitchen.

It was Bhadhra. She is in turn aback. She is searching for something.

The fright dark shape came just behind Bhadra with the knife. Devika did not understand what Bhadra was doing there.

The fright dark shape raised the knife on Bhadhra.

When it tried to impale her with the knife, Devika suddenly jumped over to the fright with a loud scream.

Bhadra was afraid and cried out with a loud voice.

After the floundering and agitation, Bhadra suddenly switched on the kitchen lights. Devika is lying on the ground. She saw the edge of the black night gown going out of the door. It flowed out and disappeared. The knife was laid on the floor.

Rice and curries are scattered in the kitchen slab. It's done by Bhadra.

Both of them stood there with panting.

Vasundhara and Indrakumar came by running.

Vasundhara (angry) to Devika: "What is this ..?"

(Pointing to the scattered rice and Curry)

Vasundhara, is trying to beat her: "you... I will... "

Indra Kumar stops Vasundhara: "No."

Indra Kumar, removed rice from the body of Devika with love.

Indra Kumar: "What's this baby ...?"

Devika diverged from him with disgust.

******

Scene - 27

Daytime

Exterior.

Devika and Bhadra came to the cage of Love Birds.

Indra Kumar's pet lovebird had been observed by Devika.

She laughs at Bhadra. She opened the cage and put her hand inside. She nuzzled the pet which is in the cage. Both of them continued nuzzling with laughter for a while.

Suddenly, Devika stopped nuzzling the bird and she remembering something.

She stood for a while and went away from the cage.

But Bhadra did not see that, because she was involved in coddling the bird.

There was an old hazed car shed in that compound which is not in use. Devika reached there.

She breaks down its rusty lock with a stone and makes the door open.

*****

Scene - 28

Daytime

Interior.

Indra Kumar is walking through the hall along with a humming of an old Malayalam song.

He found a drop of blood on the floor. Close to another blood drop. He stopped and looked it. Indra Kumar was suspicious.

There were also blood drops as a chain. Then he pursued it. It led him to the kitchen.

By kneeling down he followed the blood drops.

Vasundhara is standing in front of the kitchen slab. She is wearing a red night gown. Her night gown hoisted up to the knees. (It is not clear to the audience that it is Vasundhara.)

Her white fore leg adhere blood drops.

At that moment, Indra Kumar touched the blood drops in the ankles of Vasundhara.

She looked back screamingly with dismay.

The blood flowed through her lips and blood shrugging from her mouth. She was vociferated. Indra Kumar cried out.

Later he found bread and red sauce in her bowl.

Vasundhara: "What is this?"

Indra Kumar: "What is this, wife? Are you born to frighten a man? "

Vasundhara: "Who is hurting ...?"

Induskumar: "You've poured the whole sauce on the floor?

I thought it was blood ..."

Vasundhara is seeing the drops of sauce on the floor.

Vasundhara: "Oh, is that ..?"

Vasundhara has been made a shouted laugh. And Indrakumar also laughs.

Indras Kumar saw a special seen through the window at the distant. He concentrated on it.

With a scalawag Vasundhara applied some sauce on his nose.

Vasundhara: "My thief..."

Indra Kumar wiped it seriously and invited Vasundhara to pay attention on it.

Indra Kumar: "Oh mmm ... look at that"

They saw Devika coming out from the useless car shed.

She is holding a very old box. She walks with that.

Vasundhara: "What's in her hand? Is it a box! ... What's in that shed? I've never looked at it."

Indrakumar: "There were the cement sacks at the time of the maintenance work going on here. Then there may be a broken cot or table of Varma's Family when they lived here. I have not seen any of these boxes.

Vasundhara: "How is this girl caught it?"

Indra Kumar: "Let's ask her ..."

Suddenly Vasundhara blocked him: "No need of fight let her play with it ..."

Indrakumar comprises.

******

Scene - 29

Daytime

Interior.

Bhadra and Devika are going to the Bedroom by holding the old box. When the box is placed on the bed, in a hurry Devika locked the door.

After trying some time they opened the box. They have got only some old books, notebooks, textbooks, manjadikuru, Éclair Wrappers, a baby doll.

They watched everything with great fervor. And get an old photo. For that photo, both of them yanked.

Finally, both of them saw the photo together. A Father, Mother, a girl of seventeen year old. They were in the photo. The girl's face was blotted out.

Face of both (Bhadra and Devika) fades.

 Suddenly, knocks on the door. : "Dum...Dum....Dum...

Bhadra and Devika looked each other. Quickly they collected everything and filled the box. Both of them locked the box and pushed it into under the cot.

Then they sat on the bed as they knew nothing.

Devika went and opened the door.

It was Indrakumar.

Indra Kumar (with artificial seriousness): "I can smell a secret here!"

Both the girls are silent.

They have turgid faces.

Indra Kumar: "I knew that you got a box..."

Indra Kumar was sitting in the middle of the girls.

Girls have the same face.

Suddenly Indrakumar pulled Bhadra to him, in order to hug her.

Indra Kumar: "What are you doing here? What's wrong with you? Do not scamp to me, I am your father. "

She is struggling. Devika is watching this with anger.

Indra Kumar holds Bhadra not as a father embrace his child but as a rapist.

Bhadra twitched.

In the importune, Devika took a flower pot and hit on the head of Indrakumar.

Indrakumar felt as if his head was frozen. He left the hold on Bhadra.

Break the forehead. Blood flowed.

Bhadra startlingly passed into the corner of the bed.

Indra Kumar: "Molay ..?"

Bhadra (with fear): "go away ... go ..."

Indra Kumar (pitiable): "Molay ..."

Devika roaring like the lioness: "I tell you... get out of here".

Indrakumar quit out of the room with astonishment.

The door is closed at behind him with loud sound.

******

Scene - 30

Interior.

Indrakumar came down with the bleeding wound on his forehead. He does not understand anything.

Vasundhara sees this. She ran and came to him.

Vasundhara (with malady): "What about you? It is bleeding.

Indra Kumar (with levity): "Hmm ... stubbed on the steps."

Vasundhara (Rebellion): "If your head stubbed on the step, it won't bleed like this. It has been horrific wound. Let's go to the hospital ..."

Indra Kumar: "No, it is not serious."

He had a mental confusion rather than a wound in his head.

******

Scene-31

Daytime

Exterior.

Sit out of Indrakumar's house.

A car is passed by the gate.

The car stands in the courtyard.

The young couples got down in the yard from the car.

They were newly married couples. Shajikuttan and Bindu.

By the time Vasundhara and Indrakumar came in front of the house.

Indra Kumar's forehead had a small bandage.

Indra Kumar (with laughter): "At last you came without a call?"

Shaji: "I thought you might have a surprise too... (Looking back to Bindu); "This is Indra kumar, my Uncle... a thief; (For joke he pointing to Vasundhara) this is his wife, my Aunt Vasundhara.

Indra Kumar completed (with laughter): "The woman who feeds for thief."

Everyone laughs.

Vasundhara: "Come in."

They all got inside the house.

******

Scene - 32

Interior.

Hall.

Indrankumar, Vasundhara, Shaji and Bindu are coming to the hall.

Indra Kumar (Sofa pointed): "Sit down."

Devika and Bhadra are coming down through the stairs.

Shaji: "Oh ... come to me daughter..."

Bindhu spoke for the first time: "Indran uncle had only one daughter?"

Indra Kumar: "Yes ..."

Bindu: "Which of these is the daughter of Indran uncle?"

Indra Kumar Vasundhara and Shaji were shocked.

Vasundhara started to go to the kitchen. But she stopped and looked at Bindhu with aghast.

Indra Kumar (with doubt) said, "What did you say, Bindhu?"

Bindhu (laughter without a doubt):"I asked that, among these two girls which uncle's daughter? "

Indra Kumar (shocked): "Two girls? What are you talking about? I have only one daughter. That is she.

Shajikkuttan (A little angry with his wife): "What you know? Indran uncle had only one daughter. You're talking about somebody else? "

Bindu (suppress the impatient): "Shajiyetta, I asked who is the daughter of Indran uncle, among these two girls?"

Indrakumar (with intolerance): "Bindhu, I have only one daughter..."

Vasundhara (moving at to Bindhu with patience): "Bindu, we have only one daughter. Here there is no other girl. "

Bindhu (Feverishly): "But I can see two girls here ..."

Indra Kumar, Vasundhara and Shaji were shocked.

Bindhu looks deeply at two girls with fear.

The two girls laugh at her with a mockery.

Then they looked at her menacingly.

Interval

(Scene 32 continuation ...)

Vasundhara (feverishly): "Bindhu please say that once more?"

Bindhu (Looking at everyone in panic): "I can see two girls here. Don't you see them aunt? Don't see them Indran uncle? Can't you see them Shajiyetta...? "

Three of them looked each other.

Shaji stood up and told Indrankumar: "Come on uncle, let me say one thing"

Both of them went straight to the Sit out of the house.

******

Scene-33

Daytime

Sit out of the house.

Shaji, Indrakumar.

Shaji: "Sorry uncle ..."

Indra Kumar: "Why did you say sorry to me?"

Shaji: "There is something that I have does not tell to my uncle."

Indra Kumar: "What is the matter?"

Shaji: "There was a slight mental treatment for Bindhu. It's no problem now. She has done the Bhajan meditation in Chottanikkara temple. She was normal ... but, still...!

Indra Kumar (as Relax): "Pottada ... Onnaya ninneyiha randennu kandalavilundayorindal batha chollavathalla (A Sanskrit stave)...ha ha ha...come on ...Let's celebrate."

Shaji (with shy): "I stopped drinking"

Indra Kumar (secretly act): "This is a dialogue which all heroes are says about after marriage .... This uncle does not care about formality."

Both laugh.

Shaji (with humiliation): "Do not abash me uncle"

Indra Kumar: "Before supper ... a small ..... For company sake.... come on sun -in- law...

******

Scene -34

Daytime

Interior.

In the hall, Vasundhara stood by talking near Bindhu.

Devika and Bhadra were standing near the stair and they are listening to gusts.

Bindhu's panic mood has not changed.

Vasundhara has been struggling to relax the situation. Their body language tells that.

Vasundhara (checking the earrings of Bindhu): "The new fashion? I want to buy something like this. This is suitable for you. "

Bindu (with enthusiasm): "It is Prabhakarettan's gift...He is in UAE ... Chettan, Chechy and their children went back to UAE this morning. Mom said to me on the phone ..."

Vasundhara: "Let's call them for the next time ... We've seen them only one time."

Bindu: "Yes ..."

Vasundhara: "Oh, I will take some Coffee. Bindhu please sit down. "

Vasundhara is going to the kitchen.

Bindu was alone at the sofa.

At a distance, Bhadra and Devika are listening to her.

Bindhu tried to smile at them.

But both of them outfaced at Bindhu. With a bad shady faces, both of them approached Bindhu.

Bindhu is afraid.

Suddenly the light went off.

In faint light, Bindhu can see two dark shapes approaching her.

Bindu cried out with a loud voice.

The light came.

Shaji and Indrakumar came from the sit out, Vasundhara came from the kitchen.

Indra Kumar: "What happened?"

Shaji: "Bindu ...?"

Vasundhara: "What's the matter Bindhu..?"

She looked at everyone with terrified eyes.

Bindhu: "There is nothing ..... Nothing."

Bhadra and Devika laughed with gag and they went to the upper floor stepping the stairs.

Vasundhara looked at them with hesitation.

******

Scene - 35

At night.

The Garden.

Indra Kumar and Shaji are sitting in the chair of the garden.

Shaji: "How is life here, uncle? Uncle looks like young. "

Indra Kumar: "Relaxation for two months, dear ... these are summer holidays."

Shaji: "Oh! The best times of the UGC professors."

Indra Kumar: "How is this house?"

Shaji: "Kidilan...Marvelous! When I heard that you bought an old house and renovated,

I did not expect so much. This is like a standard resort. You can go around the world with your aunt at the time of your Vanaprastha – old age, an entertainment with money."

Indra Kumar: "An old Nalukettu. The beautiful old pond just maintained. The old owner is one sukumaravarma ... He bought it from a Namboodiri. This sukumaravarma was a misshaped man. His first wife died in a mysterious circumstance. Then he married for a second time. After that his daughter died.

And then happens the controversial murder ... The second wife has been killed and hid in the sack ..."

Shaji: "Oh ... I remember ... I have read it in news paper... That happened here. My God. "

Indra Kumar: Please be silent ... Vasundhara and my daughter did not know anything. Both are superstitious and fearful (Pedithoorikal) ..."

Shaji became something like. He looked at the surrounding darkness. He saw a white figure in the balcony. Its hair flies in wind.

Suddenly Shaji pulled out the look from balcony and drank a glass of beer and became a listener to what Indrakumar says.

Indra Kumar: "Then... do you know ... I don't have much faith in it. If we have money, let's live anywhere. "

******

Scene - 36

At night.

Interior.

Bindhu is sitting in a room of the first floor. She is just looking a book.

Camera's movement shows that someone is watching her from behind the curtain or behind the window.

Suddenly she heard some sound.

She saw, the door to the balcony just opened and closed.

She was in doubt. She got up and opened the balcony door.

There is someone standing and looking outside, wearing black nightgown.

She thought that it was Vasundhara.

Bindhu: "Aunt ..?"

There is no response from the figure. Bindhu is suffered.

Suddenly Vasundhara called from down floor: "Bindu ....!"

She turned and looked at the door with scare, and turned back to see the figure.

There was no such thing.

She was stunned and washed in sweat.

When she looked down from the balcony she saw that Indrakumar and Shajikkuttan were sitting in the garden. At a distance from there, she saw the woman who wear black night gown dragging another woman through the ground.

Bindhu looked at it. While looking at that she felt some body is standing behind her.

Bindu looked back with fear; Devika and Bhadra stands in her both side.

They stood up with dispassionate and saw that view.

Bindhu was scared.

Suddenly Vasundhara entered.

Vasundhara: "Ah ... both are standing here? Come on ... I have called you for several time ... don't you want food? "

All four walks.

******

Scene - 37

At night.

Interior.

The dishes are decorated on the dining table. Bhadra, Indra Kumar, Shajakkuttan and Bindhu are surrounded to the table.

After serving for everyone, Vasundhara sat on the chair.

All are eating rice with dishes like Chicken curry, Beef roast, Sambar, Aviyal and Thoran with Pappad.

Indra Kumar: "Is Bindu Vegetarian ..?"

Shaji: "Oh ... she does not catch the taste of tasty foods."

Bindhu looked around with suspicion when she ate.

Devika sits on the top of the kitchen slab. She is looking at Bindhu and eating something.

Bindhu looked at Bhadra. Bhadra stared at Bindhu.

Bindu looked again at Devika who was on the slab, but it was Bhadra.

Devika is sitting near the dining table.

Bindhu amazed.

Shajikkutan and Indrakumar were speaking and laughing about something.

(Music only) But Vasundhara is looking at Bindhu's expression. Wherever Bindhu's eyes went, Vasundhara looked at there.

Devika is eating at dining table and she continuously watching Bindhu. Devika's appearance changed quickly while she looked.

Bindhu realized that Devika is frightened as she saw someone behind Bindhu.

Bindhu looked back.

The back curtain flailed. Bindu saw that, two foots with blood, which were in the bottom of the curtain suddenly moved to behind the curtain.

Bindu stunned and looked at Devika. And she looked at Badhra who is on the slab.

Bhadra is vomiting over the slab. From her mouth falling something like raw meat.

When Bindhu saw it, she vomited. Everyone looked at Bindhu.

As soon as Bindhu pressed on the throat with her hand and stared her eyes as someone else pressed her throat. She has fallen from the chair to the floor. Shaji, Indrakumar and Vasundhara were got up from the chairs with anxiety.

Shaji picked up Bindhu: "Bindu ... Bindu ..?"

Vasundhara: "Mole .... Bindu ..?"

Indra Kumar called her with panic voice.

The suds and foam came out of her mouth like epilepsy.

Shaji holds Bindhu in his hands.

She was wriggling.

Immediately Indrakumar: "I'll take the car ... Let's go to the hospital ..."

Indra Kumar went out.

Carrying Bindhu in his hands Shaji runs after Indrakumar.

When Vasundhara started to run after them, she looked at Devika and Badhra.

Bhadra is eating food as it is not affected her.

Vasundhara looked at the children with hesitation and runs to the car porch.

*****

Scene - 38

At night.

Car porch.

Shaji is coming by running carrying Bindhu.

Indrakumar is starting the car of Shajikkuttan.

Vasundhara came and opened the car door.

Shaji kept Bindhu in the back seat of the car. He also got inside the car.

The car is passing through the gate.

Vasundhara looks at it.

*****

Scene - 39

At night.

Interior.

Vasundhara comes to the dining hall with hesitation and panic.

Vasundhara is looking at the vomit, debris of food that are scattered on the floor. She took the broom and dust pan and tried to clean it.

Vasundhara is sitting on the floor and cleaning.

Camera is approaching her horribly.

She is looking around with dreadful eyes.

Curtain just vibrated.

In the meanwhile, Vasundhara saw two feet with blood underneath the curtain.

She was shocked.

She remembered that there was no one to help her.

She looked at the curtain that vibrating and called loudly: "Mole ... mole ..?"

Vasundhara approached the curtain with fear.

After watching it for a few seconds, she bravely moved the curtain.

There was nothing.

She turned back with long respiration.

Suddenly she saw Bhadhra standing at behind.

Vasundhara shouted and cried out.

After a while she recovered her mental balance.

Vasundhara: "You're terrifying me."

Bhadra had a dispassionate face.

Vasundhara (arranging the vessels on dining table): "Oh! They have gone ... even without food ... everyone has gone... Oh God ... Please do not let her be in trouble ..."

Bhadra (with uncomfortable voice): "Oh ... Chumma Jada (bad act)..!"

Vasundhara (not like this): "Are you the one who made her to be frightened? She was a mentally challenged person. She was in treatment. What to say; you were sitting and eating while she was still in lethal sickness, as you do not know anything. Isn't it...?"" (As remembering) Hey, are you the one who came behind that curtain applying charcoal and blood on the body? "

Bhadra's foot was covered with long skirt.

Vasundhara in anger: "Tell me the truth."

Bhadra is looking at her horribly.

Vasundhara: "Show me your leg?"

Vasundhara is trying to lift up Bhadra's skirt.

Bhadra did not agree.

Vasundhara: "Show me your foot Bhadra. Don't make me angry. "

Bhadhra: "Please leave me..."

Vasundhara and Bhadra are making big tussle.

Bhadra pushed Vasundhara to the floor. And then, Bhadhra curled up her skirt to the thigh and showed: "Look and see this."

Her legs were clean.

Vasundhara is getting up from the floor with disgrace.

She growled strongly in order to overcome the shame.

Bhadra strongly spat on the face of Vasundhara.

Vasundhara jumped up and attacked Bhadra: "Edee ... (you)"

******

Scene - 40

At night.

Interior.

Terrible environment.

Two blooded foot climbing the stairs.

It makes the footprints of blood on the steps.

Foots were exposed from the black night gown since the gown uplifted.

There is an old kerosene lamp (lantern) in the hand.

****

Scene - 41

At night.

Interior.

Bathroom

Vasundhara with dissipated hair and a dirty face, washing her face in the wash basin.

Blood flows from her hands to the washbasin and mixing with water.

The camera moves like, someone is watching Vasundhara through the opened door of bathroom.

She also raised the night gown and washed her white beautiful legs.

Then she wiped her face with the towel and then came out.

The camera comes with Vasundhara to bedroom without cutting the shot.

She changed her night gown and worn a black gown.

Then she put make-up on her face.

Her lips became more reddish with red lipstick.

Looking at the mirror she made a cute smile.

Suddenly, the electricity has gone.

Vasundhara in a wild voice: "Damn."

She took a hanging LED light. The light made a small reflection as if it was a lantern kerosene lamp.

Vasundhara took the light. Hanging the light in her hand she walked to the hall.

Vasundhara step in the stare case with the hanging lamp.

 She uplifted the black night gown a little. It disclosed her white beautiful ankles.

Devika now revealed to the camera even though she hid herself in the shadow of the wall.

Vasundhara disappeared in the upper floor with the lamp.

Then Devika ran to the kitchen.

In the dim light of the moon, Devika burns a candle.

She burns the candle and scrabbling the corner and nook of the kitchen.

And then she groped the store room.

There was a cupboard in that room.

It was shivering.

She opened the cupboard with panic.

Bhadra was sitting inside of it. She was unconscious.

Devika pulled out Bhadra from the cupboard.

She called her with panic voice.

Devika: "Bhadra...Mole ..?"

Bhadra slowly opened her eyes.

Devika: "Mole ..?"

******

Scene - 42

At night.

Interior.

Bed room of Devika.

There was only dim light in the room.

Devika took Bhadhra and helped her to walk.

Devika helped her to lie on the bed.

She placed the candle on the table.

She swaddled Bhadra with thick blanket.

Devika looked at her affectionately.

Bhadra smiled at Devika.

Devika: "Sleep dear!"

Bhadra closed her eyes obediently.

Devika stood there for a few moments looking at her and slowly went out from the room.

She closed the door halfway.

Then she looked at Bhdhra through the gap of the door.

*****

Scene - 43

At night.

Interior.

Devika's Bedroom

Devika is watching Bhadra who is lying inside, through the gap of the door.

Devika started to scrabble to the other rooms of the same floor.

Muggiest light comes out from a room.

Devika is looking at that room.

Inside the room, Vasundhara in a black night gown sitting on the bed and checking something in the light of kerosene lamp.

It was that old box which obtained from the car porch to Devika.

Vasundhara is searching everything in doubt.

And she got that photo too. Devika's face became dark with angry.

We can see on her face the anger to tear up Vasundhara

Devika tried to do something. That time, she heard the sound of knocking at the door.

She did not understand anything.

Hearing the sound, Vasundhara raised her head and looked at the door.

She walked straight to the door with the hanging light.

She went out suspiciously. Devika hid herself there.

Vasundhara did not see her.

The knocking is hearing from the ground floor. Someone knocks on the main door.

Vasundhara steps down.

And she walked to the main door.

*****

Scene - 44

At night.

Interior.

The knock continues in the main door.

Vasundhara comes with the small hanging light.

She opens the door.

Indra Kumar comes in.

Indra Kumar: "When electricity has gone?"

Vasundhara: "Oh! Just a while before ... Where are they? Was she admitted in the hospital? "

Indrakumar (loosing the shirt's buttons): "Now she is OK. The doctor gave her two tablets. "

Vasundhara: "Then why they didn't come here?"

Indra Kumar (Shaking the shoulders): "Aah, They said ... Uncle we're going to our home. We will come another day". Vasu, there is something wrong. And I didn't compel them.

I have sent them to home and I came hither in an auto rickshaw.

Vasundhara is in tight cogitation about something.

Indra Kumar: "What do you think of? I'm hungry. Take something to eat. "

Vasundhara hold on the hand of Indra Kumar and told him.

Vasundhara: "You please come with me."

Walking along with Vasundhara, Indra Kumar: "Well, what?"

Both of them climbing stare case with the kerosene lamp light.

Vasundhara: "I have a doubt."

They never saw Devika, who hid herself in the shade of the stairs.

Indra Kumar: "Do you mean me..?"

Vasundhara (seriously): "Leave the funny jokes."

Both of them reached to the room of Devika.

Through the door that half closed, they saw Bhadra is sleeping on the bed in the light of a candle.

Bhadra's face is not clear in the shadow.

Vasundhara caught the hand of Indrakumar and took him to the room where they were sitting at first.

Vasundhara (in a low voice): "Come on."

With the help of the lamp she searched for the box in the room, but it was missing.

Vasundhara: "Oh my God, where's that box? Can that be taken away by her in the darkness? "

Vasundhara got angry.

Vasundhara: "She is pretending sleep as if not knowing anything."

Vasundhara pushed the door and entered into the room of Devika in angry with the kerosene lamp.

Indrakumar followed Vasundhara.

Scene - 45

At night.

Interior.

Devika's room.

Vasundhara and Indrakumar are coming to the room with the kerosene lamp. Bhadra and Devika are sleeping in a bed. A candle is burning on the table.

Vasundhara searched for the box under the cot with the brightness of the lamp.

The box is there.

Vasundhara pulled it out.

Vasundhara (in a low voice): "Hold the light ..."

He took the kerosene light.

The candle that was on the table blew out by Vasundhara.

She took the box and Walked out of the room.

Vasundhara (in a low voice): "Come on."

Bhadhra opened her eyes.

She is biting her finger nail and is thinking about.

After coming out from the room, Vasundhara told Indrakumar: "Get that door close correctly."

Indrakumar is shutting the door.

He walks in front of Vasundhara with the light.

Vasundhara is walking just after him with the box.

*****

Scene - 46

At night.

Interior.

In a room, Vasundhara is opening that old box.

She takes out from the box the dolls, pieces of color glass bangles, picture books, and color pencils etc...

Indra Kumar: "Is this the great treasure?"

Vasundhara looks with stare at Indra Kumar.

Vasundhara (with fury): "It's not that, this is our daughter's life ..."

Vasundhara took out a photo from the box.

In that photo there were three people. Dad, mother and a teen daughter aged fifteen.

The daughter's face was not clear.

Vasundhara showed the photo to him.

Vasundhara: "Look at this."

Indra Kumar: "Who are these?"

Vasundhara: "That's what I'm asking for. Who are these? Once we've seen her coming out from the old car shed with this box. She found this from the trash of the car shed.

Current comes at that time.

Lights and Fan started to work.

Indra Kumar: "Oh is it that box? ... Pageant of the kids."

Vasundhara (with disdain): "pageant! Coconut bunch! Every time she is there with the box opened and pampering that photo.

She's haunted like devil when she sees my face.

Now I am sure, here there is something wrong. That is why Bindhu and shajikutan has gone from here. "

Indra Kumar shocked. He immersed in strong cogitation.

Suddenly, in order to change the matter, Indrakumar said: "You say that our daughter had haunted by a ghost? Hey, Bindhu is mad. She has taken to the temple to change her madness. No need to worry about any one. Cheer up my lady. "

Vasundhara: "I'm not saying that ghosts and spooks had affected her. But we should show her to a good psychiatrist. No one knows this matter. It is necessary. If not, we will lose our daughter. "

Vasundhara stood silently for a few seconds. And then she cried.

Vasundhara: "She said that I'm her stepmother. A stepmother she never loves.

She's very angry with me. "

Indra Kumar: "You do not want to be so silly Vasundhara ... she may say something when she is angry ...but..."

Indra Kumar is pampering Vasundhara. Vasundhara His hands are shattered with angry and sad.

Vasundhara: "Do you know what she told me today? You, her father tried to rape her. I am her stepmother, a stepmother who is trying to pander her daughter to the dad. Are you satisfied? "

Indresh Kumar got shocked.

(Flash back: Devika is beating on the face of Indrakumar who is going to hug Bhadra.)

Vasundhara shouting at the ear of Indra Kumar with sad: "Or shall I believe what she said? I too have seen you are coming out from her room with a wound on your fore head that bleeding."

Indrakumar could not even speak anything for a while. His eyes filled with tears.

Indra Kumar: "She is my daughter, my own blood. She did what a daughter should not do to her father, said, what she should not say. In my mind, she is not just a beautiful damsel. She is my little baby. I still do not worry. My daughter will not say those words... "

Vasundhara: "Then why did she beat you?"

Indra Kumar did not get an answer. His voice quavered.

He went out from the room with pain.

Vasundhara is looking at him with sad.

*****

Scene - 47

Daytime

Exterior

Indrakumar approached the cage of love bird in the garden with tremor.

Vasundhara is looking at it through the window.

Indra Kumar searching the cage for his pet bird.

It is missing. That was his sweetie love bird.

He got angry.

Two or three feathers of the bird and few drops of blood were found in the cage.

Looking at the feathers he is in strong thinking.

Indrakumar is very angry at knowing who is behind the missing of the bird.

Vasundhara looked with anxiety.

Scene - 48

Day.

Interior.

Indra Kumar got into the bedroom of Devika with very angry.

Bhadra is lying on the bed.

He is holding on the hair of Bhadhra and raising her from the bed.

Indra Kumar: "Where is my pet bird?"

Bhadra: "I do not know."

Indra Kumar: "You know that. Only you know ..."

Devika is sitting on the table nearby and looking at Indra Kumar.

In the next shot, Indra Kumar is holding on the hair of Devika.

Indra Kumar: "What did you do with that bird?"

The voice of Devika is as the haunted girl.

She is growling and roaring.

Indrakumar does not let his hold on her.

Devika: "kill them ... kill them ... I will kill them again..."

Indrakumar beats Devika.

As a strong mad woman, Devika pushes Indrakumar.

In the forceful push, Indra Kumar falls into the corner of the room.

He became stagger at that attack.

Devika by running approached him like a madwoman.

For escape from her, he slipped out of the room and locked the door.

He is panting

He bathes in sweeps.

Indra Kumar, with stumbling started to step down the stare case.

Vasundhara looked up it from the bottom of the stare case.

Induskumar goes to a room.

Vasundhara is coming and leaning on the door of the room.

Indra Kumar is in a hurry to change the dress.

Vasundhara: "Where are you going?"

Indra Kumar is silent. He suppressed the anger.

Vasundhara: "What's happen there now?"

After dressing up, Indra Kumar walks out of the room and pushes Vasundhara infront of him. He is walking to the car porch.

Indra Kumar: "I want to see someone. I'll tell you things later. "

He got into the car. It's just starting.

And then he has driven away from the porch.

Vasundhara looked at it dispassionately.

*****

Scene - 49

Daytime

Exterior

Indrakumar is driving the car through the road.

On the way he stopped the car in the flank of the road.

There is a shop nearby. He is asking to the shop man.

Indra Kumar: " Where could be seen broker Lakshmanan?

A man from in front of the shop: "He had just gone here, you see him in the auto stand."

The car stands in the auto stand.

Induskumar saw Lakshman sitting in the auto with the drivers.

Indra Kumar: "Hello Lakshmanan ..."

Lakshmanan comes to the car with the familiar.

Indra Kumar: "Get in the car ..."

Lakshmanan: "How are you sir?"

Indra Kumar: "I will say. Now you get in the car. "

Lakshmanan got in the car.

Indra Kumar's car has gone ahead.

Indra Kumar: "Where does Sukumara varma live now?"

Lakshmanan: "Oh the owner of that property you bought."

Indrakumar (seriously): "Did you know about the property rightly?"

Lakshmanan says: "That's what Sir. Good property. There have good water and an old pond. Do you know what kind of property is that? What is the market price? "

Indra Kumar: "Did you know about that there was two or three transcendental death? Tell me the truth. "

Lakshmanan: "Oh my sir, native people do not go there. That Sukumaravarma does not permitted anyone to get that house. That is an old house. Death happened too much. If you're looking at superstitions, you could build a new home. "

Indra Kumar: "OK, anyway. Where does Mr.Sukumara varma live now? I have heard that he sold his property near Karmily Church.

Lakshmanan: "Oh he was leaving the region. He sold everything and he is scraggy. Now he seems to be in Poojary Nagar. It is sixty kilometers away. "

Induskumar: "Thanks Lakshmanan, get off from this car."

Lakshmanan looked around and said incredulously: "Here? This was just like the other work. How can I get back to my home?

Indra Kumar: "Get off."

Indra Kumar throws a currency of rupees 500 to him.

Lakshmanan caught it with a laugh. He is laughing with refreshment.

Lakshmanan: "OK sir, let me go."

Indra Kumar's car runs forward.

******

Scene - 50

Daytime

Exterior.

A small house.

Indrakumar's car stands in front of a small house.

It is a shabby house, but it is magnificence.

Indra Kumar came out of the car.

He pressed the house's Calling Bell switch.

The door opens.

A thirty-five year old lady with sexy look opened the door.

Woman: "Who are you?"

With a doubt, Indrakumar said, "Is it Sukumara Varma's house ...?"

The woman (disinterested): "Yes.

Indrakumar: "Is he here now?"

The woman: "Now he will come."

The woman returns to the house.

Though they did not say to sit down, Indraskumar went in and sat down in the sit out of the house.

Sukumara varma comes. He has fifty years old.

He is familiar with the words: "Oh ...... What is special? How did you find out my house? "

Indrakumar laughed formally.

Indra Kumar: "I will give you a gift. It will be a surprise for you.

Indra Kumar opened the dickey of the car and took out the box. (It was Devika has got from the car shed.)

He gives the box to Sukumara vrma with humble.

Induskumar: "I thought it was forgotten. It is a very valuable thing for you."

Sukumaravarma's face became dim.

He said: "The memories are rested in the store room in two or three boxes. However time comes, wherever it must be carried away. "

Indra Kumar: "If you have not despite, can I see the boxes?"

It is clear from the face of Mr.Sukumara varma, he did not like it.

Sukumaravarma (Looking inside): "Rema ..?"

Rema (the woman who opened the door) comes.

Sukumara Varma is going inside without talking even a single word.

Indra Kumar: " What ....Are you going?"

Indra Kumar stands aghast.

Rema: "Now you shall not stand here ..... Go fast..."

Indra kumar was angry.

Indra Kumar (Challenging): "Where....?"

Rema: "I told you to go out of here ..."

Indra Kumar (looking to Sukumara varma): "Hey, stay there. I will tell you something. The first wife was killed by the kick in her abdomen. The second wife was killed by beaten and was buried in the bag. The one and only daughter was raped and killed. (He pulled and put Rema in front of Sukumara varma) How will you kill this woman?"

Sukumara varma stopped walking and made a sudden break. Then he looked back rigorously.

Sukumara varma (with anger): "What do you want for?"

Indra Kumar (He knocking the box on the floor) replied: "Hey, you have been said that two or three boxes inside the room. I want to see that. "

Sukumara varma: "Rame ..."

Sukumara varma walks into the house.

Rama (to Indrakumar): "Come on ..."

Rema brings him to Indoor Room.

*****

Scene - 51

Daytime

Interior.

It is a store room in the house of Sukumara varma.

Rama brings Indrakumar to the store room.

There have just half luminous light.

There are some cardboard boxes and suitcases.

Dresses were pulled out of it.

Indra Kumar opened a suitcase. The silk skirts and silk blouses and other dresses were come out from the suitcase.

Rema: "He had a daughter. These are her things. "

Indrakumar got an old album.

In that album, Indra Kumar sees the pictures of Sukumara varma and his first wife.

A big picture pasted on the second page. It was the photo of Devika.

Indrakumar is looking for a long time to that photo.

Indra Kumar (Rema): "What's the name of this girl?"

Rema: "Devika."

Indra Kumar: "How was this girl died?"

Rema: "Went on the cupboard while trying to hide ... the breath was knocked out ..." (not completing)

There have the silence for a few moments.

Induskumar looks at the photo.

Rama continued: "She has come to the home for the vacation."

Indra Kumar: "Where did she study?"

Rema: "Coimbatore ... A boarding School."

Indra Kumar (with ecstasy): "In which boarding school of Coimbatore ...?"

Rema: "Anna Raja ..."

Indra Kumar (shocked): "Anna Raja ... My God ..."

Rema: "What is the matter?"

Indra Kumar (as Relax): "Nothing ... My daughter is studying there ..."

Rema: "What's the name of your daughter..?"

Indra Kumar: "Bhadra ..."

Indrakumar looked the album all out.

Indra Kumar: "Only there are the photographs of Varma's first wife and the daughter ... The second wife's photo were missing"

Rema: "Yes, It was somewhere here."

Rema is searching for the photograph.

Indrakumar (with low sound): "How did they die?"

After a short while, she told secretly: "She was killed by beaten and her dead body was buried in the bag. The people say that her secret lover has done it. My husband is poor guy. "

Indra Kumar: "How the first wife dead?

Rema: "pneumonia. Did you believe in the people's rumors? After three murders, he couldn't live like grass in our country. Do not you even understand that? "

Indrakumar is laughing with a long breath.

Indra Kumar took the photo of Devika from the Album and he said: "I am going to take it?"

She laughed with charm and said: "Oh, yes."

Both walked out of the room.

Then the camera focused to an old photo on the wall of the store room.

It is a photo of Vasundhara.

Both of them did not see it.

*****

Scene - 53

Daytime

Interior.

Vasundhara's house.

Devika, who is looking for Bhadra, walks all the way around the rooms.

Devika is stop walking with suspicious at a room of a closed door.

She looks through the key hole of the door.

Inside the room, Vasundhara is looking at the mirror for makeup.

She has worn only a brassier.

Close up her big breasts covered with brassier.

Devika shrinks her eyebrows.

Devika walks away from there and continued the searching.

She found a cupboard in a room near to kitchen.

She is opening the cupboard and she saw a sack inside it in freeze with full of blood.

Devika is crying and pulls it out from the cupboard. She unbend the sack with panic.

Bhadra was inside the sack.

She is dead.

Blood... full of blood there.

Devika is screeching loudly.

And she thought a little while.

She put there the dead body of Bhadra.

Then she runs faster.

She is going away with a heavy axe from the store room.

She is dragging the heavy axe through the floor.

Scene - 54

Daytime

Interior.

Vasundhara open the door and comes out from the room.

She is more beautiful in the make-up and lipstick.

She is wearing a black velvet night gown.

She came to the window of the hall with a humming of melody, with a smile.

She shifted the window curtains and looked at outside.

Outside the window, she enjoyed beautiful flora, old pond and trees.

Suddenly, she is hearing one of the fearsome grunts coming back.

She looks back with fear.

Vasundhara's is shocked.

Devika is standing behind her horribly and obtained with the axe.

The next moment, Devika beat strongly to Vasundhra's head with the heavy axe.

******

Scene - 55

Daytime

Interior.

Devika is walking in the rooms and she is pulling the dead body of Vasundhara.

The trickled blood of the dead body, were created marks on the floor.

There was the axe in her hand.

Devika is pulling Vasundhara's body and reaching near Bhadra's body.

Devika removed sack from Bhadra's body.

Then she is putting Vasundhara's body into the same sack.

The edge of the sack is brighter.

And she raised Bhadra's body into the cupboard.

Suddenly the sack is moving.

Devika looking that moving sack with furious and she beat strongly the sack with the heavy axe. The sack is twitched madly and then it is quiet.

Blood flows from the sack like a cascade.

******

Scene - 56

Daytime.

Vasundhara's house.

Indra Kumar's car comes home.

It stands in the porch.

Indra Kumar got out of the car and walked inside the house.

****

Scene - 57

Daytime

Interior.

Indra Kumar is coming to the hall.

There is no one there.

Indra Kumar: "Vasu...Vasundhara ..?"

Indra Kumar walks through the rooms.

Indra Kumar: "Bhadra .... Molay ...?"

He is searching for Vasundhara.

He comes to the room near kitchen.

He arrives near the locked cupboard.
No one was there, and he went back.

When something seems suspicious, he came up again, near the cupboard seems to shake up.

In the shadow of the door, Devika is lurking beside the blood shrugging sack with the axe.

She secretly sees what Indra Kumar is doing.

Indrakumar opens the cupboard with panic cry and pulls Bhadra.

Bhadra is trying to find for breath.

Indra Kumar: "Bhadra ... molay ..?"

Indukumar turned around and looked at her and said: "Vasu ... Vasundhara ... will she go down where?"

Indra Kumar pulls up Bhadra and runs with her.

Devika is looking at it.

*****

Scene - 58

Interior.

Psycological Center of Dr.Veny

Devika is sitting in the cell of the mental asylum of Dr.Veny.

Devika is wearing a white gown and covered her face with loose hair.

The cell is opened.

Two nurses brought out Devika from the cell.

Dr. Veny is standing outside with Indrakumar.

Nurses are walking with Devika through the corridor.

Dr. Veny and Indrakumar are going along with them.

******

Scene - 59

Interior.

Counseling room.

It is a spacious hall with white walls and door.

And the middle of the hall there were two chairs and a table with white color.

There have a spotlight at the top.

The nurses bring Devika to the hall and sit down her in the chair.

Dr. Veny and Indrakumar are coming there.

******

Scene - 60

Interiors.

Walking shoes are coming in the hallway in a close up shot.

Its owner is clear that he is a priest.

The priest outreach the middle age.

He goes to the counseling hall.

******

Scene - 61

Interiors.

The priest is comes to the counseling hall.

He sat on the chair against Devika.

And then he wanted to go out Dr.Veny, Indra Kumar and nurses with the look of an eye signal.

Everyone has gone out.

The priest is watching Devika.

The priest: "Bhadra ... sorry ... Devika ... all speak to Devika. I am talking to Devika. I only want to talk to Devika. "

No response from Devika.

The priest asked Devika: "Hello ..?"

Her face covered with hair.

Devika opens her eyes and looking at him between her hair.

"I am Doctor Ignatius Chunkakkaran. I am a poor priest who has to say anything with Devika. "

Devika opens her eyes and looking rigorously at him between her hair.

The priest: "Are you estrangement with me?"

After two minutes the priest asked her: "Devika, this is Bhadra's body. Not for the

Devika. Devika should go out of this body. Please go out ..."

Devika (Growing): "No ..."

The priest: "Why?"

Devika (Growing): "I love her."

The priest: "Okay. You like her. But Devika is doing harm to Bhadra now. You were gone into her body and transcend her mind and did many things like your wishes without her permission. Am I right ...? "

Devika is growing.

The priest: "Devika is the only daughter of the Sukumara varma at Kaithamanayillam. Hemambika Varma ...Your mother... A poor Antharjanam... The second bride who came into the life of Sukumara varma is your enemy Vasundhara. Ok?

Devika nods her head with fizzle.

The priest: "When you were fifteen years old, your mother Hemambika Varma died by pneumonia when you were in boarding school. Sukumara varma has not killed her.

But he did a mistake. After the death of your mother he got married his lover Vasundhara in a few days."

(Flashback Visual)

Devika has an eerie pretension.

The priest: "You did not return to the boarding. You saw Vasundhara as the cause of your mother's death. You started fighting with her. They were not too bad. She is a terrible lady...Very terrible lady.

Devika is strangely laughed like a demon.

(Flashback Visual)

The priest: "Vasundhara's lover came to your Illam (house) and started secret meetings with Vasundhara. His name was Santhosh Menon. "

Devika's face is getting worse.

The priest: "One day Vasundhara cheated you. Santhosh Menon raped you in a cruel way with the trap that Vasundhara had prepared. You decided to take revenge. During a secret meeting of happiness of Santhosh and Vasundhara, you beat Vasundhara to death and put her dead body in the sack. Santosh strike you from behind. He locked you in a cupboard. You retaliate after your death. Santhosh was killed in a road accident in Bangalore. "

The priest takes out a news paper and shows Devika.

(The news of news paper)

The priest: "Your father, Sukmaravarma, died two months ago by hanging. That is the day after Bhadra's father Indra Kumar visited him.

Devika is looking at the news paper.

The priest: "Tell me Devika, your target is completed. Now you have leave from Bhadra. You found Bhadra at the bathroom in the boarding hostel in Coimbatore. The facts that impress you are, Bhadra's mother's name is

Vasundhara and her father bought your old house. Now you have to go from Bhadra. "

Devika is growling.

The priest asked her: "Devika ... You have to listen to me."

The priest tries to touch the two palms of Devika at the table. Devika get shocked. She is trying to pull her hands for rescue.

The priest strongly holds her hands.

It is clear that a circuit travels through the hands.

The priest is holding Devika with strength.

She is twitching wildly.

Devika's face is covered with full of hair.

At the end of her twitching, Bhadra is seen in that position.

The priest took the face of the tired Bhadra.

The priest: "Mol .... Bhadre ...?"

Bhadra looks at the priest with tired eyes.

Scene - 62

Interior.

The priest comes down from the counseling room with Bhadra.

Dr. Veny and Indrakumar are eagerly coming to them.

Indra Kumar: "Mol ... Bhadra ..!"

Bhadra: "Oh my father..."

Indrakumar hugs Bhadra.

Dr. Veny is looking at the joy of father and daughter.

Bhadra's eyes fall into one who stands behind him.

That person appears to the camera.

It is Vasundhara.

Bhadra's eyes are twinkled.

Bhadra is running towards Vasundhara.

Bhadra: "Amma ..!"

But Bhadra is running towards to another woman standing beside Vasundhara.

The other woman is a pretty lady. She is Bhadra's mom.

Bhadra and her mother are hugging each other.

At that time two more people are coming there.

Shajikkuttan and Bindhu.

Bindhu is approaching Bhadra.

Bindhu calls her with doubt: "Mol..."

She is looking at Bindhu with suspicion.

Induskumar intervenes.

Indra Kumar: "This is Shajikkuttan's wife Bindhu ... They had come to our house at that time?..."

Bhadra: " What are you saying dad? I do not understand anything?"

Mother Vasundhara: "She does not remember that ...."

The other Vasundhara is standing in a particular situation.

Bindhu looks at the mother Vasundhara and the other Vasundhara.

The other Vasundhara is wearing a black night gown.

When Bindhu is looking, Devika appeared behind Vasundhara, the lady with black night gown.

Devika is looking stared at Bindhu.

Bindhu is swallowing saliva with fear.

Devika is catching Vasundhara, the lady with black night gown.

And then Devika pull her down and tweaking on floor.

She has gone and passed through the corridor with Vasundhara, the lady with black night gown.

.Bindhu is shocked.

Bhadra, Indra Kumar, Amma Vasundhara, Dr. Vani, Shaji are enjoy allocated together behind Bindhu because they did not know what she saw.

The priest is calling Bindhu with a small touch on her shoulder.

Bindhu is looking priest with aghast.

The priest is gesturing with a laugh on the face of Bindhu.

The priest: "Jim Bhum Bha ..."

Bindu sheathe her face with the hand with a little shy.

Bhadra ran with joy and pulls the hands of Bindhu and father (priest) and pulls them towards others.

The mid shot of everyone's delight moments.

The end